WILD
SUMMER

LIFE IN THE HEAT

happy yak

For Eric Maddern – living proof that there is hope in change – S.T.

Thank you to everyone who notices and then acts – A.M.

To all curious eyes who can discover beauty – C.C.

FSC
www.fsc.org
MIX
Paper from responsible sources
FSC® C016973

Q The Quarto Group

Inspiring | Educating | Creating | Entertaining

Brimming with creative inspiration, how-to projects, and useful information to enrich your everyday life, quarto.com is a favorite destination for those pursuing their interests and passions.

First published in 2022 by Happy Yak,
an imprint of The Quarto Group.
The Old Brewery, 6 Blundell Street,
London N7 9BH, United Kingdom.
T (0)20 7700 6700 F (0)20 7700 8066
www.quarto.com

Commissioning Editor: Emily Pither
Senior Designer: Sarah Chapman-Suire
Creative Director: Malena Stojić
Associate Publisher: Rhiannon Findlay

A catalogue record for this book is available from the British Library.

ISBN 978-0-7112-6972-9

Manufactured in Guangdong, China TT032022
9 8 7 6 5 4 3 2 1

WILD SUMMER

LIFE IN THE HEAT

Sean Taylor & Alex Morss

Illustrated by Cinyee Chiu

happy yak

It was rainy when Grandpa moved house.

I asked him, "Isn't summer EVER going to come?
I want it to be the holidays, so I can go and see you."

"Summer's coming," said Grandpa.
"Every time I go out, I see more butterflies.
And the foxgloves are about to flower."

Grandpa loves wild things.

"What's more," he told me. "I've found
something exciting I want to show you."

Grandpa was right.

The Sun got shinier.
The sky got bluer.
The air got warmer.

And summer came!

I asked, "Where's the thing you want to show me?"

"It's along a track I've discovered," said Grandpa. "Want to see?"

I nodded. "Shall we take your bag for finding stuff?"

"Good idea," smiled Grandpa. "*You* carry it."

As we walked, the grasshoppers sounded chirpy.
Things with wings were having fun.

Flowers stretched up, like they loved
the sunshine. And I said,
"Do plants and animals want
summer to last forever?"

"That's a good question," said Grandpa.

"And my answer is... let's look,
and see what we think.
Would this field be so full of life
if it was hot forever?
Wouldn't water be hard to get?"

I said, "There's water here!"

Grandpa looked and something shiny zoomed by.

"A golden-ringed dragonfly!" he said.
"She's a speedy insect hunter. And long hours of
summer light mean there's plenty for her to eat."

"So *she's* happy it's summer!" I said.

"Yes. Wildlife thrives at this time of year,
where a stream flows," Grandpa told me.
"But this is only a trickle now. It's maybe
because the climate is changing."

"We learned it at school," I said.
"The whole world's getting hotter."

Grandpa nodded, "That's right."

The dragonfly dipped in the stream.

I asked, "Is she the thing you want to show me?"

Grandpa said, "That's further on."

The ground was so hot I could feel it through my shoes.
"The Sun's getting strong," said Grandpa.

"I feel like being in the shade," I said back.

"Lots of plants and animals are like you," Grandpa told me.
"They find it hard being hot too long."

"Look – this snail is hiding somewhere shady. And it seals moisture in its shell by making a door of dried slime. That way it won't dry out in hot weather."

Ahead it was shady. But some of the trees were black.

"There was a fire here, last summer," said Grandpa.

"Is THIS what you want to show me?" I asked.
Grandpa smiled and shook his head.

"Fire's another reason why most wildlife wouldn't
want summer *forever*. It's natural to have a few
small fires. And fire even helps these pine trees
open their cones, which frees their seeds.
But *lots* of big fires aren't good for wildlife."

We looked at the pine cones.
Grandpa showed me new trees and flowers
starting to grow. "Life tries to go on,"
he said. "And it often has some amazing
ways of coping with dangers."

The track curved and I called out, "THE SEA!"

"Yes," said Grandpa. "And *this* is what I want to show you! They're fossils called ammonites. They might be 200 million years old! That makes them even older than me."

"You're not old, Grandpa!" I told him.
"You're only *half* old!" Grandpa laughed.

"Why are seashells up here?" I asked.

"Fossils are the remains of living things, preserved in rock," said Grandpa. "They show that where we are used to be the bottom of a warm ocean."

"Sea levels rise and fall when the climate heats or cools. So we know climate change has happened before.

But some life found ways to survive. And it's not too late to help wildlife survive in a warming world, again."

We walked down to the beach and Grandpa said,
"Those birds are Arctic terns. They're starting
one of the longest journeys any animal makes.
They'll follow the summer Sun south, all the way
to the Antarctic!"

"So THEY want summer forever!" I said.

"Yes," Grandpa told me.
"Unlike a lot of wildlife, they're able to enjoy
non-stop summer! It means they can catch fish in
sunshine and glide on warm winds, all year round."

On the beach, Grandpa said, "So, I think we've got an answer
to your question about it being summer forever.
Summer can be a time of plenty. But heat brings dangers as well."

I said, "Lots of plants and animals need to cool down too."

"Yes," Grandpa nodded. "Including me! Shall we have a swim?"

"That's a good question!" I said. "And my answer is... YES!"

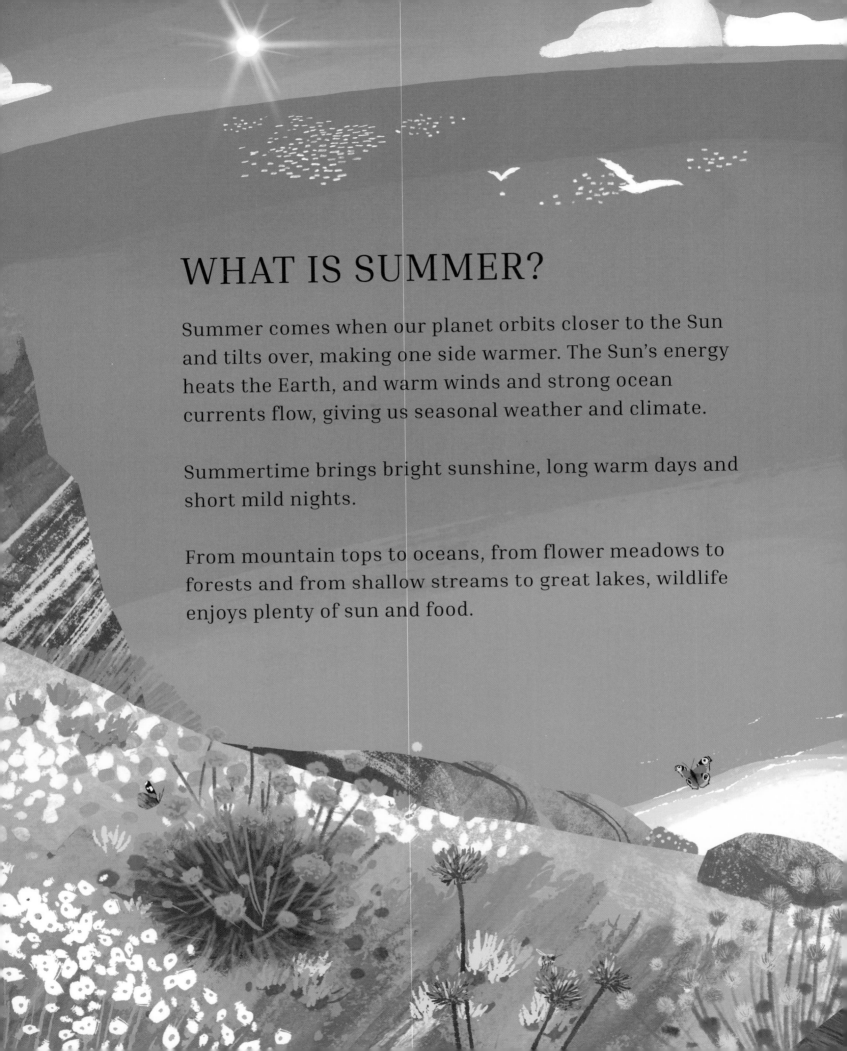

WHAT IS SUMMER?

Summer comes when our planet orbits closer to the Sun and tilts over, making one side warmer. The Sun's energy heats the Earth, and warm winds and strong ocean currents flow, giving us seasonal weather and climate.

Summertime brings bright sunshine, long warm days and short mild nights.

From mountain tops to oceans, from flower meadows to forests and from shallow streams to great lakes, wildlife enjoys plenty of sun and food.

But summer also brings drought, wildfires and powerful storms. And heat brings difficulties too.

Wildlife has adapted over millions of years of evolution to live with the changing seasons. But today the planet is warming unnaturally fast. People are putting too much carbon dioxide and other greenhouse gases into the air, by burning fossil fuels. These gases trap the Sun's heat, acting like a blanket wrapped around the Earth. And because of this, we live with more and more extreme summer weather.

LAND ANIMALS

Some land animals have evolved clever ways to cope with heat.
But many species will struggle and need to find new homes
as climate change makes summer conditions harder.

BURROWING

Burrowing owls migrate many miles to hot, summer places then move into shady tunnels left empty by small animals.

CHANGING COATS

The Arabian wolf, like many mammals, sheds a thick coat for a thinner one that reflects sunlight. This wolf also pants to cool down, and loses heat through its big ears.

HOME COOLING

Many insects and tiny creatures do well in summer, with its warmth and wild foods. But shade and water are also important. Termites stay put in all weather, building enormous mounds with tunnels and chimneys to keep fresh, cooling air flowing.

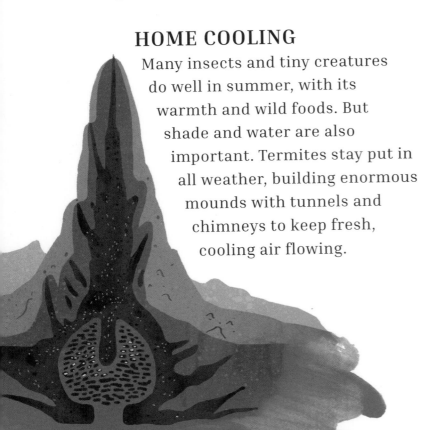

AESTIVATING

Amphibians need wet places to breed and eat. Spadefoots cope with hot, dry summers by burrowing underground to wait for rain. They go into a deep rest called aestivation and ooze goo on their skin, to stay moist.

SLOWING DOWN

Flying makes bats hot and dehydrated. Being nocturnal helps them stay cool. Some slow their heartbeat and breathing, and go into a hot summer rest called torpor. Many bats are struggling with global warming. Savi's pipistrelle can cope with getting hotter than other bats, and are increasing their range into wider areas.

AVOIDING THE SUN

Many animals avoid heat by being busiest at night, or at dusk and dawn. Red kangaroos pant, sweat and lick their fur to cool down. They took millions of years to adapt to past climate warming. However, sudden strong heat waves can stop them making babies.

WALLOWING

Wild pigs love wallowing in moist, muddy pools. Mud drying on their skin protects them from scorching Sun rays.

CATCHING DEW

Some reptiles change colour to absorb or reflect heat. And when there's no rain, lizards such as thorny devils get a drink by catching dew in tiny grooves in their scales, and it flows to their mouths.

PLANTS

Plants need good places to grow with the right amount of sunlight, water and warm air. Many plants have evolved interesting ways of coping with hot, dry summers, scorching sunshine and even fires. But climate change is making life harder for them.

ANNUALS

Many summer plants in dry places are annuals. They grow fast and live for a short time, so they escape extreme weather.

EVERGREEN

Many trees and shrubs can put up with some drought thanks to smaller leaves or being evergreen, which reduces water loss.

LEAF PROTECTION

Hairy or grey leaves reflect sunlight and help stop some plants drying out.

SUCCULENTS

Succulent plants have thick, waxy leaves or stems, to store water. Some shut their air pores by day, to stop water escaping.

BIG ROOTS

Plants with taproots or bulbs can store food and water underground. Others survive dry conditions thanks to long wide-spreading roots, which soak up more water.

DRYING OUT

Many 'resurrection plants' can safely dry out. This is called desiccation. They look dead, but they come back to life after rain.

DEFENCES

Fresh, green plants need to protect their juicy stems and leaves from thirsty animals. Some defend themselves with spines, or with nasty tastes, or poisons.

TIMING

Some plants escape hot drought by waiting underground as seeds, for months or even years. A Judean date palm seed can sprout after 2,000 years!

SUMMER MEADOWS

Summer meadow plants often have lots of flowers blossoming on different days over a long time. This increases their chances of attracting pollinators.

MOUNTAIN LIFE

Mountain-top plants, such as purple saxifrage, are among species struggling to survive global warming because they need cooler weather. When plants suffer, so does the wildlife that needs them.

SURVIVING FIRE

Plants such as cork oak, banksia trees and carnivorous pitcher plants can survive fire. They have flame-proof or heat-proof plant tissue, underground stems, or thick seed cases, and can re-sprout from ashes.

OCEAN LIFE

Summer sunlight brings new life to the sea surface, from microscopic plankton to fish, birds and mammals. All are growing and feeding. Billions of tiny ocean life forms are busy capturing carbon dioxide gas and recycling it into food and oxygen.

LEATHERBACK TURTLES

Turtles come onto summer beaches to lay eggs. Hotter sand means fewer males will hatch. And rising sea levels mean some nesting places will be lost.

SEAGRASS MEADOWS

Shallow seagrass meadows around the world's coastlines provide a sheltered summer home for a huge amount of young sealife, from tiny shrimps and fishes to birds and sea mammals. However, rising temperatures will mean less food and wildlife lives here.

CORAL REEFS

On one summer night each year, a full moon triggers a mass-spawning event. Millions of tiny young corals, fishes, octopuses and other reef life drift miles on ocean currents. Most become food, but many help create new reefs. These are homes, or places to eat, for about one quarter of sea species. But a warming climate and too much carbon dioxide is causing harmful coral bleaching on many reefs.

KELP FOREST

Kelp forests grow very fast during summer and
provide homes to a huge variety of sea animals.
Sea otters act as ecosystem engineers here. They
eat lots of sea urchins, which would otherwise
destroy too much of this seaweed.

ICY NORTH AND SOUTH POLES

The icy North and South Poles have
sunshine round-the-clock during their
summertime. The Arctic is warming twice
as fast as the rest of the world. This means
sea ice melts earlier and forms later,
making it harder for female polar bears
to build dens, find food, feed their cubs
and keep safely away from humans.

And in Antarctica, some penguin species are
changing how they breed, feed, moult feathers
and migrate, as ice melts and their world warms.

HOW YOU CAN HELP

- As summers get warmer, we can all help protect wildlife. And nature is our best friend in helping to fix global warming problems. So now it's time for us to pay more attention and act to help our planet start to heal.

- Learn as much as you can about how climate change affects wildlife.

- Use your voice and your skills to defend life on our planet and inspire others.

- Think carefully about what you buy and eat. We help protect wildlife if we buy less stuff, eat less meat and dairy and don't waste food.

- Help wildlife around you. For example, create a pond or a wildlife habitat, offer water, food and shade for wildlife, which may have lost its home elsewhere.

FIND OUT MORE

NASA Climate Kids: www.climatekids.nasa.gov/

Fossils: www.nhm.ac.uk/discover/fantastic-fossils

Discover more about ocean life: www.oceana.org/marine-life

Help wildlife where you live: www.wildlifewatch.org.uk/

A kids' guide to saving the planet: www.natgeokids.com/uk/category/discover/